Nana Gets Her
DRAGON

Written by **Helen Furlong**   Illustrations by **Joshua Allen**

AuthorHouse™ UK
1663 Liberty Drive
Bloomington, IN 47403 USA
www.authorhouse.co.uk
Phone: 0800.197.4150

Published by AuthorHouse 05/08/2015

ISBN: 978-1-5049-4202-7 (sc)
ISBN: 978-1-5049-4203-4 (e)

Print information available on the last page.

Any people depicted in stock imagery provided by Thinkstock are models,
and such images are being used for illustrative purposes only.
Certain stock imagery © Thinkstock.

This book is printed on acid-free paper.

authorHOUSE®

O nce upon a time (as all good stories begin) a little boy named Kyle was going on his first adventure with Nana. They were off to Wales to meet some friends, and to find a dragon to adopt, but just as Nana was packing the cases in the car, Kyle mentioned he had a sore throat and Mummy insisted he saw the doctor.

"Sorry young man," the doctor said. "There will be no dragon hunting for you this time. Here is some of my very tasty medicine. Take it three times a day with jelly and ice cream, and get lots of rest."

Kyle started to cry, but Nana said, "Don't worry, little man. I will still look out for your dragon and let Mummy know how I am doing, but you had better remind me what he looks like."

"Okay. His body and legs are shaped like an elephant, his paws and claws like a dog, and his tail is shaped like a crocodile's to balance him as he walks on all four paws, with his long llama-like neck held high. When he sleeps, he can curl his tail and neck around, just like next door's cat. He has stand-up scales running from head to toe, but they flatten when I am allowed to sit there to fly with my legs tucked under his bat wings. His wings are like purple silk, and they blend with his rich red colour and the deep pink under his neck and tummy. His head is cute and looks friendly, with a couple of just visible side teeth, little flared nostrils, and sparkling eyes."

Early the next morning Nana crawled out of her tent, stretched, and looked around. There was a town below and hills all about. Looking at the sky, she saw wisps of cloud appearing and disappearing over the tallest hill. Now most adults and children would think this was morning mist being blown on a light breeze, but Nana knew it was dragon's breath that was caused by the snoring beasts asleep just inside their caves.

Walking around the camp site a little later, Nana looked down onto a rough track which ended in a large circle with a lot of scorched areas.

"Hmmm," thought Nana, "This looks like the barbecue area for the camp site."

Since it was still early, there were a lot of rabbits enjoying dew-covered grass and flowers, and this made Nana realise she was a bit hungry too.

"Time for breakfast," thought Nana, and she went to join her friends, who were now up and ready. They all walked together to the camp restaurant, where they ordered a cooked breakfast and large mugs of tea. Sitting at a table overlooking the show ground, Nana and her friends tried to decide what to visit first. Just then Nana's mobile received a text. It read:

Kyle says morning, Nana, what are you doing today?

"What shall I reply?" she thought. "I know!" *Hope you are feeling better this morning. Just going DRAGON hunting!* And she pressed send.

The show was quite large. There were tents with food, crafts, exhibits, and lots of different animals.

"Now where shall I begin?" Nana thought. Looking up, she could see lots of smoke plumes at the far end of the show ground. "Ah, dragons!"

She smiled and set off at a fair pace. After ten minutes the smoke was quite close. Turning the corner, Nana gasped. In front of her was a long row of red, green, blue, yellow, and black shining smoke-puffing ...

4

steam engines!

"Oh," sighed Nana, "Not dragons, but the engines are very smart." Nana sat down at a nearby stall that was selling tea and home-made cake. (Did you know that nanas do their best thinking over a cuppa and a doughnut?) She decided to head back to camp, but first she checked all the tents in case anyone knew where she might find dragons.

The first tent had cattle on one side–brown ones, black ones, two-tone, fat, thin, and even shaggy ones. But they all gave the same answer. "Moooooooooooooooo! No we have never seen any dragons where we live."

"Never mind, and thank you all," Nana said and headed over to the other side of the tent.

This side was much noisier than the first. Grunts, snuffles, and even squeals filled the air. Looking around, all Nana could see were hundreds of pigs of all kinds. There were large pink clean ones, small white dirty ones, bristled ones with straw hanging from their ears, hungry ones with their snouts in a food trough, and a very large mummy pig with sixteen babies sleeping by her side.

Nana decided to ask the mummy pig. "Do you know where I could find any dragons at this show?"

"Oink, oink," replied the mummy pig. "Apple sauce and hog roast! Are you trying to start a riot? We hope there are no d-r-a-g-o-n-s anywhere near here."

"Sorry," Nana said, leaving before she upset the pig any more.

The next tent was full of sheep and lambs. Some had thick wool, some had no wool, some had two horns, and some had four. There was even a queue of sheep waiting for a man to take their coats off with electric clippers. They all gave Nana the same answer.

"No, no. You must be baaaarmy if you think we would go anywhere near those terrible creatures."

"Ah, my favourites!" Nana smiled as she turned to the other side of the tent. Horses and ponies filled the area, tied in long lines. It seemed they came from all over the world. There were horses from Arabia, Portugal, America, Russia, and Britain.

"Do you know of any dragons around here?" Nana asked a rather tubby but pretty Welsh pony that she thought might have some knowledge of the local area.

"Neigh," laughed the little pony. "Don't you know dragons are like unicorns, invented by adults to amuse their children?"

Nana sighed and moved on to the very last tent. She was beginning to realize that finding a dragon for Kyle might not be as easy as she thought. This tent had a notice outside that read "Poultry and Pets". Nana looked around hoping to find some pet dragons on display. There were flocks of birds chirping, squawking, and quacking, lots of furry rabbits, mice, rats and guinea pigs, but nothing that looked like a dragon.

Disappointed, Nana asked her question one last time, but she got the same sort of reply.

"Why ask us?" said a daft-looking duck with a pompom of feathers on its head. "All birds have feather brains. We don't know what a dragon is or what they look like."

Nana turned to go, wondering what she would tell Kyle when she got home.

As she walked towards the exit, a small brown rabbit ran to the corner of its cage, stood on its back legs, twitched its nose, and called out to her.

"Nana, don't give up yet! I heard what you've been asking, and I know someone who can help."

Nana walked over to his cage, sat down, and looked at the rabbit.

"Did you see the rabbits on the track by the camp site this morning? Well, they are my relations. I suggest you have a word with my cousin Catkin in the morning as she seems to know everything about the local dragons.

"Thank you," said Nana, feeling very excited. She dug around in her pocket for a carrot.

(Nana always carried a carrot around just in case. It's the sort of thing nanas keep in their pockets, along with tissues, sweets, rubber bands, toy cars, and so on. You never know when they will be wanted.) Thanking the young rabbit, she headed back to the camp and her tent to relax and wonder what the next morning would bring.

When Nana awoke the next morning, the sun was shining and there were no clouds to be seen over the surrounding hills. After a quick breakfast of honey sandwiches and a large mug of tea, Nana left her tent. When she walked down to the track, she could only see one lonesome rabbit, and it didn't seem very happy.

Nana looked at her watch for the first time that day and realized it was nearly ten o'clock. No wonder the rabbit was impatiently tapping its paw!

"Good morning. Sor ..." Nana got no further.

"Oh, I thought you weren't coming. You're very late, considering that it's Wish Day," muttered the rabbit.

"Wash day?" said Nana. "I'm sorry if you're busy. I had no idea."

"*No*, not wash day! *Wish* Day!" The rabbit corrected her.

"I'm a little confused. It sounded like you said 'Wish Day'. I'm having trouble understanding your accent. But that makes no sense at all!"

"You did hear right," said her little furry friend. "I can't explain now. You will have to come to my house, and we can chat over tea and cake. It must be nearly ten o'clock."

Off the rabbit hopped down the slope, calling for Nana to follow. A couple of minutes later they were in a little dell, outside a large rabbit hole.

"Sorry about the rush. Please do come in. My name is Catkin. My cousin sent a message saying you might call. He had forgotten it was Wish Day. Follow me, but mind your head, and I'll put the kettle on."

Nana found herself in a lovely cosy kitchen-diner and was surprised she had no difficulty standing.

"It must be something to do with fairy-tale houses and animals. This rabbit seems about the same size as I am. Or am I the same size as the rabbit? Very confusing!" thought Nana.

Once tea and fresh carrot cake were on the table, Catkin was ready to talk.

"Now, I understand you are interested in dragons, so I shall tell you all I know, and then you can ask me any questions if you like."

"That's fine," said Nana, taking a small sip of dandelion tea.

"Well," said Catkin, "to start at the beginning, a group of dragons are known as a 'dragoon' when they are on the ground, but when they are flying, they are called a 'drift' of dragons. Babies are always born during the first week in June from rainbow-coloured eggs. The first present any dragon receives is a life cloak that has been lovingly knitted by the eldest grandmother of the dragoon, using her extra-long index claws. The 'wool' is a mixture of moon dust, star shine, and cobweb thread. This allows them free movement when they are away from their enchanted hill-top homes.

"During the first three months of a dragon's life, they are confined to their hill-top settlement. At this age they are multi-coloured and cannot fly. Later, they change into their adult colours, the rarest being red and the most common green or blue. This is because, if you want to blend in, there is lots of grass, trees, sky, or water to disappear into. But oh dear! If you're *red* there is a shortage of poppy fields. Telephone boxes and post boxes are too small. Fire engines are a better size, but they have a nasty habit of dashing off, leaving a dragon feeling rather embarrassed and exposed!"

Catkin continued. "Young dragons are not allowed to fly solo until their first birthday, and they have to pass a very strict flying test. Not only do they need to pass the test, but they must also complete fifty flying hours with a qualified family member. Baby dragons are fluffy all over, but they can grow prematurely scaly if they are not regularly cuddled enough. They only drink water when young—definitely no fizzy drinks are allowed—and fire breathing is discouraged in the first twelve months.

"All dragons of any age must eat three charcoal biscuits a day to keep their furnaces burning. If they eat one or two extra, there is enough excess energy to heat their caves, bath water and cooking stoves.

"Dragons *do not* eat humans—fresh or tinned. Their favourite snack is hot dogs (the sausage kind) with plenty of fried onions and whole-grain mustard. They eat vegetables by the kilogramme, and they adore vegetable kebabs made with large cabbages, cauliflower, marrows, carrots, and swedes. They like these bar-be-cued, and they eat them whole."

"Dragons are named after the first strong characteristic they show after birth. At the moment, the local dragoon leader is called Majestic 4326th. This is rather a mouthful, and it is said his wife calls him Fred as it is shorter!

"The only other thing I know about dragons is that when they are grown up, they love dandelion and burdock pop and they buy it by the barrel." Catkin poured them both more tea and cut two large chunks of cake.

"Any questions?"

"Well," said Nana, "A few things come to mind. First, what language do dragons speak? Second, is it possible to adopt young dragons? And third, what did you mean by 'Wish Day' when we met earlier?"

"Ah," said Catkin, settling back in her armchair and reaching for her carrot cake. "Speaking dragon is not a language as such. It's more like a thought. If you truly believe, you just think you are speaking to a dragon, and if there is one nearby and they want to, they will answer you inside your mind. That way, all conversations are private and can't be overheard.

"Adoption was stopped centuries ago. There were lots of cruelty cases brought before the Society for the Prevention of Cruelty to Dragons (or S.P.C.D.) involving the canned humans. I think you call them knights.

"Now Wish Day happens once a month on a Thursday, when it is early closing down in the town. It is the day when our local dragons come to do their shopping and that day is today!"

"Once they have all arrived safely," Catkin explained, "they chat and catch up on the month's news, views, and gossip. They like to exchange recipes and discuss the antics of the eggling dragons. The main subject today will probably be the dragoon birthday party and flying award ceremony at the end of the week.

"They will have an early lunch of hot dogs and kebabs and will leave about two o'clock to go to town under their life cloaks (of course) so they don't scare the natives and tourists. Each dragon carries a shopping list and drops it in a box by the town hall. All orders must be placed by three o'clock. Majestic 4326th then opens a second box by the town hall and takes out a pile of wishes that the town folk have dropped there. One of these will be chosen as 'wish of the month' as payment for their supplies. The dragons then return to their landing site to discuss the wishes, removing those that are thought to be selfish, silly, or duplicated and a vote is taken. This is why it is locally called Wish Day.

"Putting a wish in the box might be a good way of finding out about dragon adoption."

"If you are in time and really believe in dragons, you will see which box to put your wish in. If not, you will only see flower pots.

"Now I am sorry to rush you on your way, but time is slipping away very quickly, and I have my burrow work to do. I have to make a carrot and corn pie big enough for forty-two rabbits, as I have a few close relations coming for dinner tonight."

Nana stood up and asked Catkin if there was anything she could help with. Catkin told her that everything was under control, so Nana left the burrow, which immediately returned to normal rabbit size as she put her feet on the path.

Nana turned left down the track which led to the town at the bottom of the hill, hoping she would be in time to place her wish in the box and buy some fresh food for her lunch or tea. Looking back up the hill, Nana thought the air seemed very heavy and rather cloudy, not to say shimmery. "Dragons are arriving," she thought to herself and hurried on her way.

The town didn't seem very big, but some of the shops were larger than usual. The pet shop seemed to have sacks and sacks of charcoal biscuits in some very strange flavours, such as sausage and onion, roast vegetable, and even chilli pepper and garlic—surely not the taste of your average pet poodle!

There was a large warehouse built behind the greengrocer's shop, and today it seemed to be over flowing with enough fresh vegetables to feed the county for a month. Halfway down the high street on the left, between a small chemist's and an even smaller optician's, Nana did notice one unusual shop. The name read in large letters over the door, "Bangers R Us". On inspection, it seemed to sell nothing but hot dog sausages and various sauces, all of which sounded very hot and spicy.

As Nana walked on towards the town hall, she did her shopping. At the baker's she bought a couple of fresh loaves labelled "Dragon Bread". (She was told by an assistant that it was a local bread very similar to her usual tiger bread.)

At the dairy she purchased a pint of gold-top milk, half a kilo of freshly churned butter, and a kilo of welsh cheddar.

The last shop she went into was the small supermarket at the corner of the town square. The assistant looked nervously at her watch as Nana entered. Nana started to look around, but after a few minutes, the lady behind the counter spoke to her. "Is there anything I can get you? It's early closing, and I must leave in a few minutes."

"Just the local paper, some aspirin, and a pack of cherry tomatoes, please. Oh, and I'll have some of the dandelion and burdock pop, as you seem very well stocked."

"Would that be a barrel or a bottle?" said the assistant with a smile.

"Just a bottle please," laughed Nana. She paid the lady and left the shop. The time was 12.57.

As she looked back along the street, all the shop signs were turning to "closed" and the doors were locking as if by magic.

"Now to find the wish box," thought Nana. She crossed the road to study the flower displays outside the town hall. "I hope my belief is strong enough," she thought, staring at the flowers.

On the right she saw a box marked "List", while on the left stood a smaller box that read "Wish". Nana dropped her wish into the left-hand box, and she glanced back in time to see the boxes disappear. In their place were two large pots of multi-coloured snapdragons. The air in town was getting a lot warmer, and there were patches of heat haze up and down the street.

The air was cooling as Nana climbed back up the hill. She passed the dell where Catkin lived. The rabbit waved as she finished cleaning the windows, and when she opened the burrow door an amazing smell of fresh carrot and corn pie escaped that made Nana feel really quite hungry.

When Nana reached her tent, she put her shopping in a cool box, deciding to eat later. She took a sun-lounger, the paper, a chilled glass, and her bottle of pop to the nearest sun trap and settled down for a relaxing afternoon.

Now Nana didn't know it, but she was only about a metre away from the local dragon chief, Majestic 4326th and his flying fledgling Chuckles, his great-great-great-grandson. They were lying under their life cloaks. Majestic was relaxing with his eyes closed. Chuckles couldn't settle.

"I'm bored," moaned the young dragon.

"Settle down, young lad," sighed Majestic. "I need some rest if I am to test you on your flying skills to see if you can fly solo after your birthday party tomorrow night, and it won't be too long before we have to sort out the wishes."

Meanwhile, Nana had drunk a glass of pop. She put the paper over her eyes and started to drift off to sleep. Her last conscious thought was that the rumbling she could hear must be a distant thunder storm.

"I'm still bored," Chuckles said again, but this time he got no reply.

"I'm thirsty," Chuckles said, but all that came from Majestic was a whoosh of steam and a rumbling snore.

A little later Chuckles thought, "I really am thirsty. I'll just peep out carefully and see if we are near any water."

Chuckles carefully lifted his cloak and cautiously peered out. He could not see any water, but he did see Nana dozing in her lounger with an open bottle beside her. Chuckles carefully lifted the bottle and took a long slow glug of the brown liquid. The bubbles shot up his snout, which nearly made him sneeze. Though the bubbling sensation was a bit weird, Chuckles liked the taste—and it had made him less thirsty.

He put the bottle back, checked that no one had seen him, and curled up with Majestic for 37.5 winks.

Chuckles woke after thirty minutes (or thirty winks in dragon time) with a very strange feeling in his tummy. He tried lying in various positions, but none seemed comfortable. He decided to sit up, and that was when his troubles started.

He burped.

It was not a quiet little burp but a *large* dragon-sized burp that made him spurt a large ball of flame through his nostrils. Had he not been sitting between Majestic's *enormous* front feet, things might have worked out okay. But he was, and things were about to get worse.

Chuckles burped twice more.

Each time a ball of flame landed on Majestic's outstretched left foot. Majestic let out an agonised scream, which frightened Chuckles into losing his burps.

"Ow! Ow! Ow! OW! ouch! What have you been up to now, young dragon?" asked Majestic, waving his foot about and blowing on it.

"Nothing, nothing at all," replied Chuckles, quaking with fear.

"Are you sure? I vaguely remember you muttering you were thirsty a while ago. Have you drunk anything you shouldn't have?"

"Oo heck!" said Chuckles. "I'm sorry. I looked for water, but I couldn't see any. Then I spotted a bottle of brown liquid by this nice-looking human's chair. It's alright. She was fast asleep. As I am only a day away from my birthday, I thought it wouldn't matter. It would save me troubling you. It was very nice, and, and, and ..." Here Chuckles started to sniff, and little tears appeared like sparkling diamonds in the corners of his eyes.

"Oh, I'm getting too old for this mentoring job," muttered Majestic. "Now calm down, young Chuckles. What is done is done. We will just have to sort things out. First let's see if I can stand on this foot."

It was no good. Each time he put any weight on it, his face turned a nasty shade of green, causing him to gasp and sit back down.

"Now, young dragon, as I cannot fly at the moment, you are going to have to run down to your Great Great-Great-Uncle Grim 2444th and ask him to supervise the take-off for home and arrange for my shopping to be stored in my cave. Then explain about my foot. Tell him that we will stay under the cloak until it feels less frizzled. Off you go now. And watch what you are doing! I think you have caused enough trouble today. Remember, absolutely *no* flying."

"Okay, Grandad. I will remember."

Chuckles shot out from between Majestic's feet. He was eager to please his chief, but as soon as he was clear of the cloak he knew he was in *big big* trouble again.

Out in the sunshine, Chuckles realized his mistake: he was not wearing his life cloak. And there, wide awake and smiling at him, was Nana.

"Hello, little dragon."

The little dragon turned his head back in the direction he had come from and called out, "Great-great-great-grandpa Majestic, I think I am in even bigger trouble now."

"What have you done now, young chap? It can't be that bad! You only just left less than a wink ago."

"It's alright," thought Nana. (She remembered what Catkin had said: dragons use a thinking language, not a speaking one.) "I quite believe in dragons, and if you have a problem, I'd like to try and sort it for you." (That's the sort of thing nanas do best.)

"Hmm." A gruff voice popped into Nana's head. "I wouldn't normally ask for human help, but young Chuckles here seems to have landed us in a bit of a pickle."

The air around Nana shimmered. Very cautiously, a huge scaly head appeared about three metres off the ground. Then, once Majestic had checked for dangers, he let the life cloak slip slowly off the rest of his body, revealing that Nana had actually put her lounger in the centre of his back and was virtually surrounded by curled up dragon!

"My, my! What a magnificent dragon you are! I am so pleased to meet you. Would you be the Majestic 4326th I have heard so much about this morning?"

"Yes," said Majestic, "You seem very well informed for a human."

"Ah, indeed," said Nana. "I spent the morning with young Catkin Rabbit, being educated."

"That explains it. The keeper of the runway. I always thought she was a bit of a gossip, but maybe it is for the best."

"Now what are these problems I might be able to help you with? But do you mind if I sit down? My neck is rather stiff looking all the way up to you, sir."

"By all means!" said Majestic. "I shall rest my head on this boulder, and then we should both be comfortable. As for you, young dragon, sit here! Do not move or even breathe heavily if you think anything else might go wrong!

"Well, Nana, as you know, today has been our shopping day, and we are now waiting for its delivery so we can fly home. Unfortunately, young Chuckles here got thirsty while I was having sixty winks. I do get a little tired these days; after all I am 276 years young tomorrow. So he sorted it himself by drinking some of that bottle." Majestic pointed to the now half empty bottle of dandelion and burdock.

"Oh, that's not a problem. I don't mind sharing. Oh, hold on! Didn't Catkin say something about young dragons and the drinking of pop?"

"Yes," sighed Majestic. "As he has not had his first birthday yet, he has not been shown how adults drink liquids with bubbles, and there lies the start of our problems."

Majestic continued to explain. "He allowed the bubbles of pop to heat up while he slept. This made him very uncomfortable, and he burped three times, each time letting off a ball of flame which has badly burnt my foot. *Look!*" Majestic held his foot up for Nana to see.

"Ugh! That does look painful, and there are a few nasty large blisters coming up". (And a very nasty smell as well, which Nana decided not to mention).

"Now what are we going to do? You see, vertical take-off is not possible for us larger dragons. We have to take a good long run and then jump as we reach maximum speed to get airborne, and I can't even put the slightest bit of pressure on this foot. Chuckles was just going to run down and find his uncle and arrange for our shopping to be taken home. We will have to stay here for a couple of days until my foot is better, but there is always the danger of being discovered–especially with young Chuckles being so energetic and, of course, being *red*. Not all humans are as friendly as you, Nana."

"Okay, give me half an hour–or I suppose you would say thirty winks–to think of a plan. Meanwhile I suggest you cover up again. I can hear a couple of cars turning into the camp site. I'll leave you a bottle of chilled spring water for you both, so there won't be any more accidents."

It took longer than she had thought to think of a plan and persuade her friends to go out for the evening without her, as some of them (Glynis, Heath, Pat and Ruben) would be heading home the next day. She claimed she had a terrible headache. (Nanas can tell fibs if it's a matter of life, death, or burnt dragons). Eventually they all left. After waiting ten minutes, Nana went back over to her lounger, loaded down with her shopping from town and the bag she always had near her for emergencies.

"It's all clear. You can come out now!"

The two dragons appeared, and they watched as Nana took the items she wanted out of the bags and put them in front of her on the grass. There was a pack of sticking plasters (with dinosaurs printed on the front), the packet of aspirin, one of the loaves and a bread knife, two more bottles of chilled water, and half the butter she had bought from the dairy.

"Oh," thought Chuckles, "Nana has got us a picnic tea. That would go down rather well! I always get hungry waiting for the shopping."

"No, Chuckles, this is not a picnic. This will, I hope, get you both home for your tea tonight."Chuckles looked at the items again and looked very puzzled.

"Right, Majestic, let's have a closer look at that foot."

First Nana washed it with a bottle of spring water. At least it would smell a little fresher now! Then she took the bread knife, which made Chuckles go rather pale.

"It's alright, Chuckles. I'm only cutting the bread, not cutting Majestic's foot off!"Chuckles was getting very confused. He sat scratching his head with a back claw as he watched.

Nana measured the loaf against Majestic's foot and used the knife to trim it to size. Next she picked up the butter.

"I hope this doesn't hurt too much, Majestic," she said. She started to smother the burnt bits of his foot with great big dollops of greasy butter. She sliced the ready trimmed loaf in half lengthways and carefully sandwiched the foot between it. Then she took the plasters and stuck the two halves together to make a rather strange-looking shoe.

"There you go," said Nana. "Try standing on your foot now."

Majestic stood up and slowly put his weight on his foot. There was a sharp intake of breath and then a dragon-sized sigh.

"A lot better, thank you. But what made you have such an unusual idea?"

"Well, my mum always said to cover burns with butter to take away the ouch, and I thought the loaf would give you something soft to protect it while you ran. If it's still aching a bit, there is another hour or so before you fly. I would suggest you take this bottle of water and swallow ten of these aspirin. I'm not sure of the dosage for dragons, but I'm sure that ten won't do someone your size (no offence) any harm, and they should take the worst of the pain away. Then you can rest while I amuse Chuckles for you."

While Majestic snoozed quietly, Nana and Chuckles first played hide and seek, but this was too easy for Nana. No matter how well Chuckles hid, there was always a tip of red tail, wing, or foot to give away his hiding place. Then they played a game of I-spy, and Chuckles won, as Nana's eyesight was not as good as the young dragon's.

Majestic woke at four-thirty when he heard the rumble of lorries and vans coming up the hill towards the runway."Here, Chuckles, time to go," he called. "Thank you, Nana, very much for fixing things for us. I agree nanas are very good at fixing things. Now, is there anything I can do for you before we leave?"

"Well, I must admit I put a wish in the box earlier today, but could you possibly toast a couple of slices of this bread and melt some cheese on them, as I am feeling a little hungry?"

"No problem," said Majestic. Within minutes he had made a dragon-sized portion of cheese on toast.

"Mm, that smells wonderful and looks just how I like it—golden brown with crisp singed bits round the edges."Nana gave her young dragon friend a slice to munch before he flew home, as he was eyeing the plate and his little pink tongue was chasing around his lips. Then with a wave and many a thank you, the dragons disappeared under their life cloaks and were gone.

After the dragons left, Nana poured the remains of the dandelion and burdock into a glass and sat in her lounger to rest for half an hour or so. She read the local paper and ate her perfect cheese on toast.

Just before six o'clock, the side of the hill was hit by a cooling breeze that seemed to come and go in pulses, and Nana realised that the dragon drift were flying home. She shaded her eyes and looked into the breeze, hoping to see her new friends, but there was not even a wing tip to be seen. Nana collected all her things and headed back to her tent. The bag of useful things was packed behind the front passenger seat of her car, so she knew where it was. The remaining bread, butter, cheese, and tomatoes she packed in the cool box along with the milk. She then shook out her sleeping bag in case any creepy crawlies had set up home, collected her wash bag and a big fluffy towel, and headed for the shower with a set of clean clothes, as she was sure she could still smell burnt dragon foot!

By nine o'clock Nana felt cool, relaxed, and clean. Her friends were just returning to camp, so she went to make cocoa for them all (with plenty of marshmallows, of course).

When they had all had a large mug of cocoa, they sat out in the evening sun and discussed what they were going to do for the rest of the holiday. It was decided that they would go to a nearby castle which was open to visitors. There was a guided tour available of the castle and grounds and an orangery restaurant overlooking the crashing waves that hit the cliffs below.

The evening was meant to be warm and fine, so a barbecue would pass the time. According to the local paper, there would be a colourful light show over the hills if the sky was clear. This happened each year around this date, always on a night in June, and no scientist could explain it. But if the night was clear enough, it was really spectacular.

"Party on, dragons," thought Nana, but her friends didn't hear her as she was thinking in dragon!

The next morning Nana and her friends all had breakfast together, and then they waved goodbye to Heath, Glynis, Pat, and Ruben who were heading for home. Then they headed off to explore the castle. The weather was glorious, and the day passed quickly. They even found a farm shop selling everything they would need for their barbecue. They returned as the sun was starting to lose its heat and was thinking of its bed!

The fresh farm food was absolutely yummy, and they settled down for a night of chatter and, they hoped, a wonderful light display. The multi-coloured lights raced across the sky, twisting and turning, chasing but never colliding.

"Just like a Red Arrows display, but without the planes," said one of Nana's friends. They went to bed early, as they were planning to head for home the next morning, but the lights continued across the sky for a long time after they had gone to bed.

As she settled for the night, Nana thought what a wonderful party her dragon friends must be having. She hoped that young Chuckles had passed his flying exam and learnt to drink pop safely! With these thoughts she fell into a relaxing sleep.

The last morning was dry, but there was a lot of mist over the hills that stopped the sun fully shining through. Nana woke suddenly, sure she had heard someone clearing their throat at the base of her bed. Sitting up, she looked around but could not see anyone.

So she decided that now she was awake, she may as well get dressed. The noise came again a little louder this time and seemed to be inside her head.

"How very strange! Perhaps my friends are trying to scare me."

"It's me! Look at the end of your bed," said a little voice. Nana saw a bright red snout, which was quickly followed by the rest of Chuckles, who was wearing a great big grin. (This was a little scary, as he had so many shiny white teeth!)

"Hello, young friend. I wondered if I would see you before I left for home. Did you have a good party last night?"

"Fantastic," said Chuckles. "I have never been allowed up so late before." He tried to hide a great *big* dragon-sized yawn. "Did you see our flying display, Nana?"

"Yes, I thought it was ever so good. My friends enjoyed it too, but they had no idea what caused the light show. Does this mean you can fly solo now? I don't think Majestic is with you."

"Yes, I came top of the year with 203 per cent, and Majestic gave me a letter to bring you this morning. These days he tends to need a really good lie-in after a really big party." Chuckles dropped a large white handkerchief into Nana's hand. "Read it, read it," he said, jumping up and down and making the bed shake.

"Manners, young Chuckles!" cried Nana, hoping her friends couldn't hear the kerfuffle.

"Sorry, I got a little excited. Please would you read the letter, Nana?"

"No, sorry, Chuckles, I can't. I don't know how," She turned the large handkerchief over and over in her hand.

"Oops, my mistake! I was meant to explain. Dragon letters are magical. When you are ready, I shall blow lightly on it to release the letter, and then you can read it aloud as the words scroll to the top where they evaporate. That way, anyone finding it by mistake only finds a handkerchief."

Nana settled next to Chuckles and said she was ready. This is what she read once the young dragon had opened the letter:

Dear Nana,

Firstly I must thank you for sorting my foot, which is now totally healed and in record time. I have suggested all mummy dragons keep bread and butter in their first aid kits, as we do tend to have a few similar accidents each year. Now to let you know we have discussed all the wishes for this month and have chosen the one from the local teacher wishing that the church can raise enough money for its new roof at the coming fête. We did however like the idea of your grandson adopting one of our dragons - a wonderful idea. And so this wish has also been passed by the committee as an extra thank you for all your help. If you are agreeable, Chuckles will be the first, and while he is with you and Kyle, he could sort out adoption for his peers. He will also be able to teach Kyle the ways of any mythical, magic or fairyland characters he may have questions about. If you agree to this, Chuckles will send us a smoke signal to let us know he has been adopted, and then can teach you how to care for a dragon and check that he has perfected his disguise.

Yours magically,

Majestic 4326th

And then the handkerchief went blank.

"Oh, yes please!" said Nana, turning towards where Chuckles was sitting, but he wasn't there anymore. In his place was a red fluffy soft *toy dragon!* But when she looked really closely, the dragon winked!

"Oh, a nearly perfect disguise! But you will have to be careful about that wink ." I think my friends are ready to go to breakfast, and then when we're safely at the café, you can send your smoke signal home. Right, let's see if your disguise passes this test."

Just then, Nana's friend Emma popped her head round the tent flap.

"Are you all packed and ready for breakfast? Gosh! What a splendid dragon. Is it for Kyle? I wish I'd seen one, I could have given it to Grace for Noah's first soft toy. It almost seems real. I even thought it winked at me, but it must have been a trick of the light. Are you coming with us for breakfast? We are about to walk over."

"Yes, I'm coming," said Nana, giving Chuckles a quick secret smile.

It was early afternoon by the time everyone had packed their cars and said goodbye. Emma thought it very strange that Nana insisted the toy dragon wore a seat belt in the front of her car, but then Nana was a little odd sometimes!

"Off we go, Chuckles! It won't take us long to get home."

But there was no reply. The car's movement had already rocked the little dragon to sleep.

Just before they entered the little road where Kyle lived, Nana pulled over and made sure Chuckles was wearing his life cloak and that he knew to stay hidden and quiet until Nana was ready for Kyle to meet him.

As Nana turned into the drive, Kyle, his friend Liam, and their mums Carley and Heather were just arriving home from the shops. On spotting the young boys, Chuckles started to bounce up and down on his chair, making the seat look alive.

"Sit down and stay quiet please," thought Nana as she opened her window.

"Hello," called Nana. "You look a lot better than when I last saw you, Kyle. Are you all better now?"
Yes, thank you, Nana. Are you going to join Mummy and me for tea? It's cheese on toast today."

"Yes, I'll join you for tea, but can you help me unload the car? There are some tomatoes, milk, butter, cheese, and bread that need to go in your mum's fridge."

When Kyle carried the box in, no one noticed a shift in the air as someone had mentioned cheese on toast. Before Nana locked the car, she told Chuckles where the charcoal biscuits and water were, and she told him she would be back soon.

There was no reply, so Nana assumed he was asleep again. She went into the house for a much needed cup of tea and cheesy toast. Kyle was in the kitchen jumping up and down. He was excited to see Nana and had so many questions to ask her.

"Did you? Has it? Were you? And if you did can ...?"

"Kyle, sit down and let Nana have her tea in peace. I know you have a lot to ask her, and I'm sure she will answer all your questions after we have all eaten."

Kyle knew it was no good arguing with his mum, so he sat quietly and started to eat a slice of cheese on toast. After a few minutes, when there was a break in Nana and Mummy's talking, Kyle spoke.

"I know Mummy told me to wait, but can I ask one question? I am a bit worried."

"Alright, go ahead."

"Well, can anyone else hear a sort of crunchy noise in their head?"

"Now you mention it, yes," said his mummy; Nana just looked thoughtful.

"And can anyone explain why the slices of toast are marching in a line and disappearing near the edge of the table by that empty chair?"

They all looked at the table. They all looked at the toast. They all looked at the empty chair. Both Mummy and Kyle looked puzzled, but Nana sighed.

"Well, I did bring a friend home to meet you. He was meant to be waiting in the car." Nana looked at the empty chair. "I think you had better come out and meet the rest of the family, don't you, Chuckles?"

Kyle blinked hard and smiled.

"You found a dragon, Nana, but he is only a cuddly toy. So why was the toast moving?" The toy seemed to look at Nana, and she nodded and said, "It is quite safe. We all love dragons here."

With that, Chuckles became his real size. Kyle gasped and jumped down from the table and ran round to give the dragon a big hug.

"Can he stay?" asked Kyle hopefully.

"Yes—as long as Mummy agrees and you come and finish your tea while I tell you the whole story from start to finish."

Or should that be from start to the beginning? I will let you, the reader, decide.

Lightning Source UK Ltd.
Milton Keynes UK
UKIC01n2237040615
252933UK00009B/65